DISNEY

CLUB PENGUIN ™

PICK YOUR PATH 1

Stowaway!
Adventures at Sea

Grosset & Dunlap

DISNEP

CLUB PENGUIN™

PICK YOUR PATH 1

Stowaway!
Adventures at Sea

by Tracey West

GROSSET & DUNLAP
Published by the Penguin Group
Penguin Group (USA) Inc., 375 Hudson Street, New York,
New York 10014, USA
Penguin Group (Canada), 90 Eglinton Avenue East, Suite 700,
Toronto, Ontario M4P 2Y3, Canada
(a division of Pearson Penguin Canada Inc.)
Penguin Books Ltd., 80 Strand, London WC2R 0RL, England
Penguin Group Ireland, 25 St. Stephen's Green, Dublin 2, Ireland
(a division of Penguin Books Ltd.)
Penguin Group (Australia), 250 Camberwell Road, Camberwell,
Victoria 3124, Australia
(a division of Pearson Australia Group Pty. Ltd.)
Penguin Books India Pvt. Ltd., 11 Community Centre, Panchsheel Park,
New Delhi—110 017, India
Penguin Group (NZ), 67 Apollo Drive, Rosedale,
North Shore 0632, New Zealand
(a division of Pearson New Zealand Ltd.)
Penguin Books (South Africa) (Pty.) Ltd., 24 Sturdee Avenue,
Rosebank, Johannesburg 2196, South Africa

Penguin Books Ltd., Registered Offices:
80 Strand, London WC2R 0RL, England

© 2008 Club Penguin. Used under license by Penguin Young Readers Group.
All rights reserved. Published by Grosset & Dunlap, a division of Penguin Young
Readers Group, 345 Hudson Street, New York, New York 10014. GROSSET &
DUNLAP is a trademark of Penguin Group (USA) Inc. Printed in the U.S.A.

Library of Congress Control Number: 2008029487

ISBN 978-0-448-45055-1   10

"I can't believe Rockhopper is back on Club Penguin!"

Snow crunches under your flippers as you walk to the Beach. You and two of your buddies are headed to the *Migrator*. A few days ago, you spotted the pirate ship in the telescope on top of the Lighthouse. Today you read in the newspaper that Captain Rockhopper docked his ship. He's having a one-day-only party onboard, and you are not going to miss it.

"Do you think we'll get to meet Rockhopper?" your green buddy asks. He is decked out in striped overalls and an eye patch for the party.

"I heard if you meet him, he gives you something special," says your pink friend. She's wearing pirate gear, too: a red pirate dress and a black pirate hat.

"That would be awesome," you say. You, too, are dressed in your pirate best. You're wearing a red and black striped pirate shirt that you got for free at one of Rockhopper's parties. And you've got a red pirate bandana around your head. "Almost as awesome as getting to sail on the *Migrator* with Rockhopper."

"What do you mean?" your pink buddy asks. "Nobody gets to do that."

"Didn't you read that book in the Book Room?" you say. "Bambadee got to sail with Rockhopper. He stowed away onboard."

"Of *course* I read that book," says your pink buddy. "Don't you remember how it ends? Rockhopper brings Bambadee right back to Club Penguin."

"That's right," your green buddy points out. "Even if you stowed away, Rockhopper would bring you right back here."

You know your friends are probably right. But that's not how it happens when you daydream. You imagine becoming Rockhopper's best friend, sailing the seas together and visiting all kinds of mysterious places. You've always wondered where the pirate gets those amazing items he brings back to Club Penguin. And what about all those glimmering jewels he has in the *Treasure Hunt* game?

"If I hid carefully, Rockhopper wouldn't find me," you say. "I could wait until we're far out at sea. Then it would be too late for Rockhopper to turn back."

Your pink friend stops. "You have a funny look in your eyes," she says. "Are you seriously thinking about stowing away on the *Migrator*?"

You pause. You've thought about it a lot, but you hadn't made up your mind until now. "Yes!" you say, and a sense of adventure fills you from the top of your penguin head to the tip of your penguin feet. "I'm going to do it!"

Your pink buddy looks nervous. "You'll need a plan," she says.

"I know," says your green friend. "We can distract Rockhopper while you find a good hiding place."

"That just might work," you say. You have been on the ship before, so you know your way around. You're sure you'll find a good place to stow away.

The three of you turn a corner, and the *Migrator* comes into view. Rockhopper's party is in full swing. The Penguin Band is on the deck, playing sea chanteys. The deck is crowded with penguins dancing and talking. You walk up the gangplank and join the crowd. Then you look up at the tall main mast and see Yarr, Rockhopper's red puffle, bouncing up and down on top of the sails.

"There's Yarr!" your pink friend says. "I wonder if that means Rockhopper is here."

You look around the deck, but you don't see the pirate captain. "Let's check belowdecks," you suggest.

You walk down a flight of steps into the Ship's Hold. It's just as crowded as the upper deck. Giant barrels of cream soda, Rockhopper's favorite drink, are stacked against one wall. The main attraction is a colorful green and orange tent that holds treasure Rockhopper has brought back from his travels. This time, he is giving away a free item—a pirate belt. You grab one and put it on. He also has a cool furniture item for a sale—a porthole that would look great in your igloo. You know you have enough coins to buy it, but you have to focus on your goal—looking for a hiding place!

"Hey, let's play *Treasure Hunt*!" your green friend calls out.

You can't resist. You waddle over to Rockhopper's quarters. It's a mess of pirate equipment: telescopes, treasure maps, treasure chests, and a bunch of instruments you've never seen before. A portrait of Rockhopper and Yarr hangs above the captain's desk.

But the most exciting thing in the room is the *Treasure Hunt* game. Small sandboxes are scattered across the floor. You and your buddies grab a shovel and find an empty sandbox. Then you take turns playing the two-player game, digging in the sand to uncover hidden jewels. You're all racking up the coins when you hear a familiar voice above deck.

"Ahoy, me hearties! How do ye be likin' my party?"

"Rockhopper!" your friends squeal, and you quickly hurry back above deck. Rockhopper is there. You'd know him anywhere: He's bright red with a black beard, bushy black eyebrows, and a black captain's hat on his head. Penguins swarm around him, eager to meet him. You see that each penguin walks away with a signed photo of the captain.

"No way! I want one!" your pink buddy cries. Your two friends rush up to meet Rockhopper, but you hang back. You don't want to draw any attention to yourself.

When Rockhopper is done making friends, he cries out, "Aaargh! Let's dance!" The band begins a rousing tune and you can't help yourself—you've got to dance!

You are having so much fun dancing that you forget all about your plan to stow away on the ship. Then Rockhopper yells out, "Party's over, mateys! Me and me trusty puffle Yarr have got to heave-to and set sail tomorrow, and I need me sleep!"

You start to panic. You forgot to find a hiding place! You're not sure if you want to go through with your plan, but your green friend grabs your arm.

"We'll keep Rockhopper busy," he says. "Find a good place to hide."

"Good luck!" says your pink buddy.

You nod. You can't back out now. Your friends run off to talk to Rockhopper, and you look around. There are some crates over there by the rail. Maybe you could hide in those? You waddle toward the crates.

Then you hear Rockhopper's voice. "No more pictures, lads. I've got to get me sleep!"

You quickly duck behind the main mast.

Rockhopper is escorting your friends off of the ship. There's no time to run for the crates. The staircase is just a short hop away. You could scoot down there and find a place to hide in the Hold. Or you could shimmy up the mast and hide in the Crow's Nest. Rockhopper would never look there!

If you run down into the Hold, go to page 15.
If you climb up into the Crow's Nest, go to page 53.

"Let's take the path on the right," you say.

"Aye!" Rockhopper agrees. He and Yarr follow you down the path.

The path leads you to the edge of the zucchini fields. Up ahead is a large grass hut. You are so excited! You run inside.

The hut is filled with clay puffle statues!

"Wow, these are cool," you say. "I'd love to have one in my igloo."

"I'm sure that other penguins would love to have one, too," Rockhopper says. "Let's haul this onto the *Migrator*. These statues will make a mighty fine treasure to sell."

The iguanas help you load up the ship. They are sad to say good-bye to Yarr.

"Bye! Bye! Puffy! Puffy!"

You wave good-bye to the iguanas and set sail for Club Penguin. You can't wait to get home. Your friends will be excited to see the new item you're bringing back!

THE END

CONTINUED FROM PAGE 67.

You remember what Rockhopper told you earlier. "A sense of adventure is a pirate's most important tool." You realize that if you're going to be a pirate, you need to do the adventurous thing.

You run down the gangplank and catch up to Rockhopper. He looks pleased to see you. Yarr bounces up and down, excited.

"Ahoy, matey!" he says. "Glad you're up for an adventure."

"Can I help you look for sailing equipment?" you ask.

"Me and Yarr here will check to see if there's a port on the other side of the island," Rockhopper says. He hands you a canvas sack. "Why don't you go look for fruit trees? I've had a hankerin' for some tasty fruit lately."

You nod and rush off. Rockhopper has given you a job! Better yet, you get to explore the island.

You head down a path into the jungle. You're used to snow and ice on Club Penguin. Here, there are green plants as far as you can see. Giant pink and orange flowers bloom on vines. Colorful butterflies flit from plant to plant. You scan all of the trees as you go, but you don't see any fruit growing on them.

Then the path splits and goes in two different directions. You stop. Should you take the right path, or the left path?

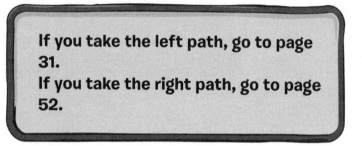

If you take the left path, go to page 31.
If you take the right path, go to page 52.

CONTINUED FROM PAGE 11.

You're not sure if you can climb up the mast fast enough, so you quickly rush down the stairs. It's dark down there now, and you squint, trying to find a place to hide.

Suddenly, you hear loud footsteps overhead. Rockhopper's voice carries down the stairs as he sings an old pirate chantey.

"Sixteen penguins on a treasure chest! Yo ho ho and a bottle of cream soda!"

He's coming down into the Hold! You've got to hide, fast. But you're not sure where to go. You think you can see the barrels of cream soda ahead of you. With your flipper, you feel an open doorway to the right of you. Maybe you should duck in there.

If you hide behind the barrels of cream soda, go to page 27.
If go through the doorway, go to page 37.

CONTINUED FROM PAGE 58.

You decide to try to set the sails without Yarr's help. If you do it right, Rockhopper might let you stay onboard his ship. Of course, it's a longshot, but you have to try.

You gaze up at the mast. Four sails are tied to the mast with rope. You need to raise the sails so that they can catch the wind when the ship sails. You know that much, at least.

You shimmy up the mast. It's not easy. You almost reach the rigging when you start to slide down. Panicked, you grab for a rope.

The rope quickly unravels. You let out a yelp as the rope carries you back down onto the deck. The sails fall on top of you. You groan.

"Havin' some trouble, are ye?" It's Rockhopper. He heard your crash from belowdecks. He pulls the sails off of your head. The sea turtle is behind him, grinning. You're so embarrassed!

"Uh, yes," you say, blushing. But Rockhopper doesn't get angry.

"I'll just set the sails meself," he says

pleasantly. "Why don't you give our guest a tour of the ship?"

That you can do. "Let's start with Rockhopper's quarters," you tell the sea turtle. "There are lots of cool things to see in there."

"That sounds nice," the sea turtle says, and the two of you head belowdecks.

You enter the quarters and point to the *Treasure Hunt* game. "Everybody on Club Penguin loves playing that game," you say. "Do you like to play games where you live?"

The sea turtle doesn't answer you. You turn, and see the turtle is standing on Rockhopper's desk with a gleam in his eye.

"Consider yourself tricked!" he says. He reaches into his shell and pulls out a fake beard and an eye patch. He quickly puts them on. "I am Captain Shellbeard, famed pirate of the seas! I pretended to be lost so Rockhopper would rescue me and I could come aboard his ship."

Shellbeard swipes a treasure map from Rockhopper's desk. "This is my treasure now. Ha ha ha!"

He jumps off of the desk and trips, landing on his face. You run after him but before you can grab him he jumps through the porthole.

"Shellbeard strikes again!" he cries.

You look out of the porthole. There is a rowboat below with three turtle pirates! Shellbeard is swimming toward them, carrying the map above the water.

Your first instinct is to jump overboard and stop Shellbeard from getting away. But that seems kind of dangerous. You should probably get Rockhopper, but you're afraid of what he'll say when he finds out you've been tricked.

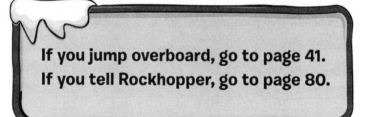

If you jump overboard, go to page 41.
If you tell Rockhopper, go to page 80.

CONTINUED FROM PAGE 55.

"Hmm. Snakes can move very fast. Maybe that's the answer to the riddle," you say.

"You've been right so far," Rockhopper says.

You head down the path marked with a snake. The path twists and turns. You go left, then right, then left again. The sun shines brightly overhead. Yarr is so exhausted, it can barely bounce. Rockhopper takes off his hat and wipes the sweat off of his head.

"We're in some kind of maze!" he cries.

You're afraid Rockhopper is right. Then it hits you—snakes wriggle, they don't run. But a river—a river runs! It's so obvious. You took the wrong path.

"Let's keep walking," you say. "I'm sure we'll find a way out."

You try to sound positive, but you know the truth. You're hopelessly lost!

THE END

CONTINUED FROM PAGE 45.

There's no time to run down into the Hold!
You quickly grab the life preserver shooter.
You've used one before. When you pull the
trigger, a round life preserver shoots out,
attached to a long rope. You figure if you can get
the life preserver around one of the monster's
horns, you can pull it away from the ship.

You aim and shoot! The life preserver almost
reaches the monster's head, but falls short. The
rope tangles around the monster's neck.

ROAAAAR! The creature cries out and
dives underwater, trying to break free. The ship
starts to turn upside down. What have you done?

Luckily, Rockhopper wakes up just in time.
He releases the life raft. You, Rockhopper, and
Yarr jump down into the raft just as the *Migrator*
disappears under the water.

"It's all right, matey," Rockhopper says. "I'm
sure someone will rescue us."

You look out over the wide, empty ocean and
hope Rockhopper is right.

THE END

CONTINUED FROM PAGE 64.

"Let's try the top of the anchor," you say.

Rockhopper nods and steers the ship to the top of the island chain. The wind is in your sails, and you soon see the first island. Rockhopper slows down and begins to search for the passageway.

Suddenly, you hear a screeching, scraping sound against the hull of the ship. You look over the side. "Rocks!" you yell.

The water here is filled with jagged rocks. The *Migrator* is wrecked. You have no choice but to jump into a life raft and head for shore.

"We're shipwrecked!" you moan.

"Not for long," the Guide says cheerfully. "The Host will send a rescue party. In the meantime, did I tell you about the time I guided a group of dolphins to an underwater cave?"

You sit back in the sand and listen as the Guide and Rockhopper trade stories of their sea travels. It helps to pass the time while you wait for the rescue party . . . and wait . . . and wait . . .

THE END

CONTINUED FROM PAGE 58.

You don't want to risk making another mistake, so you ask Yarr to help. There are four sails tied to the mast, and you need to unfurl them so they will catch the wind. Yarr jumps from rope to rope so you know which ones to pull. Soon, the sails are set.

"Thanks, Yarr!" you say.

Rockhopper is pleased to see the *Migrator* is ready to set sail. He and the sea turtle have looked at maps and figured out how to get to the sea turtle's home.

You sail the sea all day and all night. The next morning, Yarr scans the horizon with his telescope. He starts to bounce up and down.

"Land ho!" Rockhopper cries.

"Home sweet home!" says the sea turtle.

The *Migrator* docks, and you all walk down the gangplank. A group of sea turtles is waiting.

"Look! Our audience member has returned. And he has brought new audience members with him!" a turtle says.

"Audience members?" you ask.

Another turtle holds up a sign that says

APPLAUSE and the turtles all start clapping. You look at Rockhopper, confused.

Your friend the sea turtle walks up to a turtle with a blond wig and a microphone.

"Let me introduce you to our Host," the turtle says.

Now you are more confused. "Host? What do you mean?"

The Host smiles at you. "Thank you for returning our audience member. Why don't you wait in the Green Room until the show starts?"

You want to ask what a Green Room is, but it's no use. The turtles usher you, Rockhopper, and Yarr into a hut with a couch, a TV, and a table with a plate of vegetables and dip.

"What is this place?" you ask.

"It's mighty strange," Rockhopper agrees.

You turn on the TV set. It's tuned to a game show channel. You change the channel, but all you get is static. It's the same with every channel. Only the game show channel comes through on this island. You think you are starting to figure things out.

"Host. Audience. Green Room," you say. "They think life is one big game show!"

A sea turtle carrying a clipboard walks into the hut. "The show's about to start. Follow me."

You follow the turtle out of the hut onto the Beach. The Host is standing in front of rows of folding chairs, filled with sea turtles.

"These two brave penguins and one little, uh, fuzzy thing, have rescued our audience member!" the Host says. "It's time for them to choose their reward!"

A turtle holds up the APPLAUSE sign again, and everyone claps.

The Host turns to Rockhopper. "What will it be?" she says. She points to the side of the stage area. "Will you choose what's in that sand pit, or what's inside the hut?"

Rockhopper looks at you. "Hmm. I think there may be treasure here, matey. Which should we choose?"

If you tell Rockhopper to choose what's in the pit, go to page 51.
If you tell Rockhopper to choose what's in the hut, go to page 63.

CONTINUED FROM PAGE 42.

You walk to the door and open it—and find yourself face-to-face with a turtle pirate! You should have checked to see if the door was guarded!

"The prisoner is loose!" the pirate yells. He marches you upstairs. Shellbeard is there, and he looks angry.

"Our prisoner can't be trusted," Shellbeard says. "It's time to walk the plank!"

He points to the gangplank leading down to shore.

"Okay," you say. Shellbeard is letting you go!

"Oops! I meant *that* plank!" Shellbeard says, and this time he points to the plank jutting out over the water.

You gulp. You look for another way to escape when a large snowball flies through the air and knocks into Shellbeard! The *Migrator* has found you. Yarr is shooting the turtle ship with snowballs from the cannon.

Rockhopper swings down onto Shellbeard's ship on a rope. He grabs you around the waist.

"This is how a *real* pirate does things!"

he says. Then he swings you back onto the *Migrator*.

"Thank you!" you say.

Rockhopper shakes his head. "I'd best be getting you back to Club Penguin."

When the *Migrator* docks, a reporter from *The Club Penguin Times* is waiting for you. She writes a story about your rescue called "The Sorry Stowaway." It's kind of embarrassing, but at least it makes for a good story!

THE END

CONTINUED FROM PAGE 15.

Suddenly you remember that the only door in the Hold leads to Rockhopper's quarters. That would probably not be a safe place to hide. So you run for the cream soda barrels and hide behind them.

You hear Rockhopper's footsteps and peek out from behind the barrels. He yawns and stretches and then walks into his quarters. Yarr hops along behind him. Rockhopper closes the door, and you sigh with relief. He hasn't seen you!

Your heart starts to pound. You've done it! You've stowed away. Now you need to think of a great place to hide so Rockhopper won't find you until he's far, far away from Club Penguin. Maybe you can sneak out and explore the Hold when Rockhopper is asleep . . .

Meanwhile you yawn. It's been an exciting day, and you're tired! You close your eyes, just for a moment. And, the next thing you know, you are hearing a deep voice above you.

"Well, what do we have here, Yarr? It looks like a stowaway!"

You open your eyes to see Rockhopper

standing over you. You fell asleep! You must have been sleeping a long time, because the door to the Hold is open, and sunlight is streaming down the stairs.

"I-I can explain," you stammer.

You're afraid Rockhopper is going to be angry, but instead, he grins and pats you on the head. "Blimey! You've got a sense of adventure, I see. I felt the same way when I was a little lad. I've got saltwater running through me veins!"

"Does that mean I can sail with you?" you ask hopefully.

"Of course not!" Rockhopper chuckles. "I sail alone. Except for me puffle, Yarr, of course."

Behind Rockhopper, the red puffle jumps up and does a somersault in the air.

You sigh. "I understand."

"Don't be so sad, matey. Come on deck with me. Ye can watch me steer the ship back to Club Penguin," the captain tells you.

You follow Rockhopper up the stairs. But when you get to the upper deck, he stops and frowns.

"Ahoy! A storm be brewin'! I wasn't expectin' this. I'm afraid ye'll have to go back down below. It's the safest place," Rockhopper tells you.

You see the black clouds swirling in the sky, and you don't argue. You run back down to the Hold.

The storm kicks up quickly. Your stomach lurches as the *Migrator* rocks back and forth on the wild waves. The items in Rockhopper's store fall out of their crates and spill onto the floor. You grab onto a heavy treasure chest and hang on.

The storm rages on for hours. Finally, things become calm. The ship isn't rocking back and forth anymore. You decide to venture above deck to see what's going on.

Rockhopper is steering the ship. His captain's hat is dripping with rainwater. He takes it off and dumps the water on the deck.

"Is the storm over?" you ask.

"Aye!" Rockhopper replies. "But now we're in another pickle, matey. The *Migrator*'s been blown off course!"

Go to page 47.

CONTINUED FROM PAGE 54.

You decide that you and Yarr should stick together. You both climb down from the mast and leave the ship. You quietly follow the iguanas, hiding behind palm trees as you go.

The iguanas take Rockhopper to a village full of tiny grass huts. They speak to each other in fast, high voices in a language you can't understand.

"Snicker doodle oh!"

"Kicky! Kicky!"

They put Rockhopper into a cage and slam the door shut. They fasten a padlock on the door handle. The cage looks flimsy, like it's made of bamboo poles. You look down at Yarr, thinking fast. You know Yarr loves bowling, especially if it's the bowling ball! But, maybe you should try and rescue him yourself.

If you bowl Yarr into the bars, go to page 39.
If you sneak up to the cage and try to pick the lock, go to page 62.

CONTINUED FROM PAGE 14.

You decide to take the left path. It leads you to a clearing. There are fruit trees circling it, loaded with a strange-looking green fruit. The fruit is round with little bumps all over it. But it's definitely fruit.

You start to pick the fruit when you notice a stream flowing behind the trees. There's something sparkly in the stream. You bend down to get a closer look and see that the stream is filled with sparkly stones! Could they be valuable jewels?

You're not sure what to do. Rockhopper only gave you one sack. Should you fill it with fruit, like he asked, or bring him the sparkly stones instead?

If you take the green fruit, go to page 43.
If you take the sparkly stones, go to page 61.

You decide to shoot Yarr out of the cannon.
After all, he likes it! So you stuff the barrel with
gunpowder, light the fuse, and hold your ears.

BOOM! Yarr flies through the air with a
happy look on his face. He lands right in the
middle of the group of iguanas.

You watch as the iguanas step back and
stare. They are all quiet for a moment. Then
they begin to talk rapidly in some strange
language.

"*Zoom! Zoom! Puffy! Puffy!*"

"*Zookeenee! Zookeenee!*"

They all bow to Yarr! Then they untie
Rockhopper. They motion for Rockhopper and
Yarr to follow them.

"Let's go, Yarr! Me sense of adventure is
calling!" Rockhopper says.

You are curious to know what the iguanas
are up to. You scramble down the mast and race
off of the ship. You follow the iguanas down a
path that leads through a jungle.

The path opens up into a village of small
huts. In the center of the huts is a huge, clay

statue of a puffle! The clay is a reddish color, and the statue looks just like Yarr.

"Wow!" you say.

Rockhopper turns to look at you. "A penguin in a pirate shirt? What are ye doing here?"

"Um, I stowed away on your ship," you say.

"Shiver me timbers! This day is gettin' more interestin' by the minute," Rockhopper says. "Stick with me, matey, until we find out what these lizards want with us."

Just then the crowd of iguanas parts, and another iguana walks in. She is wearing a headdress made of yellow flowers and is carrying a book.

"Zoom! Zoom!" the iguana says, and hands the book to Rockhopper. You watch as the pirate captain opens the book. Inside are crudely drawn pictures. The first picture shows a puffle falling from the sky. Then the puffle lands in a field of some kind of vegetable—a zucchini? Then the zucchini grows very big, and the iguanas do a happy dance.

You look around and notice that large fields of zucchini surround the village. "I think the iguanas think that puffles bring them good luck," you say. "They think puffles give them a good zucchini harvest."

Another iguana walks in front of Yarr and puts a small treasure chest in front of him. You help Yarr open the chest. Inside is a piece of paper—it looks like a treasure map!

"It's written in our language," you say. "There's a map, and there are riddles on it."

"Looks like they're givin' Yarr some kind of reward," Rockhopper guesses.

"Zoom! Zoom! Puffy! Puffy!" the iguana leader says.

You and Rockhopper look at the map. The starting point begins at the start of the zucchini field. You and Rockhopper and Yarr walk to the starting point. You head down the main path. Then you notice that the path forks in two. There is a rock in front of each fork. One rock has a picture of an iguana on it. The other has a picture of a table.

"I think we're supposed to solve the riddle to figure out which way to go," you say. "Here's the first riddle. What has four legs but can't walk?"

If you choose the path marked with an iguana, go to page 46.
If you choose the path marked with a table, go to page 55.

CONTINUED FROM PAGE 55.

"Snakes wriggle, but rivers run," you say. "Let's take the path marked with the river."

You head down the path, and you don't get far before the road forks again. You look at the map and read the riddle.

"What kind of bow cannot be tied?" you read. "I know this one. It's a rainbow!"

You look down at the rocks marking the paths. But there's a problem. The sun has faded the markings so that each rock just has some squiggles on it. Neither one of them looks like a rainbow.

You frown. "What do we do now?"

"We forge on, matey!" Rockhopper says, putting a flipper around your shoulder. "We can't turn back now. Let's pick a path and find our treasure!"

If you take the path on the right, go to page 12.

If you take the path on the left, go to page 68.

CONTINUED FROM PAGE 15.

You duck into the doorway. You're not sure what room you're in, and you still can't see very well. But you see a large piece of furniture, and you climb into the space underneath it. Your heart is pounding.

The gentle rocking of the ship puts you to sleep. You've had a long night, and you can't help yourself—you fall asleep.

You wake hours later to a strange sound.

Zzzzzzzzzz! Zzzzzzzzzz! Zzzzzzzzzz!

It sounds like—snoring! There is sunlight streaming into the cabin, and you look around and see the *Treasure Hunt* game. You're in Rockhopper's quarters and that's the sound of Rockhopper snoozing away! You need to get out, fast, before Rockhopper wakes up.

You climb out from under Rockhopper's dresser and tiptoe across the floor. You almost reach the door when you feel something soft and furry bounce on your head.

"What was that?" you cry out.

You look down. Yarr is hopping on the floor next to you, smiling. Rockhopper sits up in bed.

"By my beard! A stowaway!" he yells.

"I can explain," you say nervously.

"There'll be no explainin'. There are no stowaways on my ship, period. I'm takin' you back to Club Penguin," Rockhopper says. "I'm on a mission to find a special chain of islands shaped like an anchor. I've heard vast treasure can be found there. I can't be havin' any distractions."

Rockhopper climbs out of bed, puts on his captain's hat, and stomps up to the top deck. You follow him. You've definitely made him grumpy.

You remember some great jokes you read in the Club Penguin newspaper. You decide to tell him one. But suddenly, you see something shining in the distance off the side of the ship. Rockhopper is looking straight ahead. He doesn't see it.

If you tell Rockhopper about the shining in the distance, go to page 56.

If you tell Rockhopper a joke, go to page 73.

CONTINUED FROM PAGE 30.

You decide to use Yarr as a bowling ball. You pick him up by the top of his fuzzy head and roll him toward the cage.

Slam! The flimsy bars break open. You rush in and quickly untie Rockhopper. He looks shocked to see you.

"I stowed away on your ship," you say. "I'll explain later. Now we need to get out of here."

"Yucky! Yucky! Zoom! Zoom!"

You look behind you to see an angry group of iguanas holding zucchinis. You don't think it would hurt to be hit with a zucchini, but you don't want to find out, either.

"Let's go!" you yell.

You head into a jungle path. It is thick with vines and branches. You push your way through, hoping it will lead to shore. Instead, it leads to the top of a waterfall.

"Blimey!" Rockhopper says. "This is a real jam we're in, matey."

Yarr jumps off the path, onto a pile of fallen logs. He starts to pretend he's surfing.

"I think Yarr wants us to surf down

the waterfall," you say a bit nervously. The waterfall looks steep—and dangerous. You look around.

"Yarr! There's another path here," Rockhopper says, pointing. "But it may lead to another dead end."

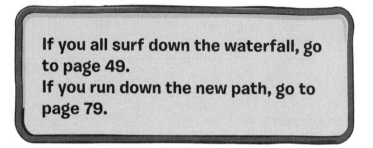

If you all surf down the waterfall, go to page 49.
If you run down the new path, go to page 79.

CONTINUED FROM PAGE 18.

You jump through the porthole and splash into the water. You swim and catch up to the boat. The trouble is, you have no idea what to do when you get to the boat.

You climb onboard and angrily wave your flippers. "Give me back that map!"

Shellbeard laughs. "Ooogh! What do we have here?"

"'Ooogh'? Don't you mean 'Aaargh'?" you say.

"Whatever," Shellbeard replies. He straightens his fake beard. "Get him, men!"

Before you can swim away, the three turtle pirates grab you. They drag you into the rowboat and tie a rope around you. Then they row to another small island, where Shellbeard's ship is hidden away in a cove. They march you into the Hold.

"Let's see how much treasure Rockhopper will give us for your safe return!" Shellbeard says. Then he slams the door to the Hold and marches above deck.

You are alone in the Hold. You pull at

your ropes, and they easily come off. These pirates don't seem to be very good at their job.

You've got to escape. You waddle over to the porthole and look down. All you can see below you is ocean. You could jump and try to swim for shore. Or you could sneak up on deck, grab a lifeboat, and jump overboard before the pirates catch you.

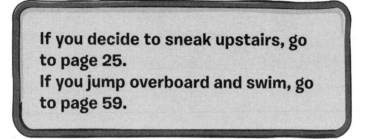

If you decide to sneak upstairs, go to page 25.
If you jump overboard and swim, go to page 59.

CONTINUED FROM PAGE 31.

You decide to fill your bag with fruit, since that's what Rockhopper asked for. Then you head back to the *Migrator*.

Rockhopper and Yarr are standing on the shore.

"Ahoy there, matey. I'm afraid me and Yarr couldn't find a port anywhere. This island be deserted," Rockhopper says. "We'll have to sail on and try to find our way back to Club Penguin."

"I found some fruit," you say, and open up the sack. Rockhopper seems pleased.

"It's been so long since I've had fresh fruit!" he says. He picks up a piece of the green, bumpy fruit and takes a bite.

"Shiver me timbers!" he cries. He throws the fruit over his shoulder. "That be tastin' fouler than a moldy sweat sock!"

You feel terrible. You've failed again! Then you notice something. The fruit rolls across the sand and knocks into something. You dig in the sand a little bit and pull out a sextant that's been washed on shore! It's in perfect condition.

"Well, what do ye know?" Rockhopper says. "Let's set sail, then. To Club Penguin!"

You put the sack of green fruit in the Hold. It's a souvenir from your trip, at least.

Exhausted, you drift off to sleep in your hammock. Rockhopper says you'll land on Club Penguin soon.

But something wakes you up before then. It's a strange, loud roar. You race above deck. Rockhopper is at the wheel of the ship. Something splashes out of the water.

It's a sea monster! The creature has a body like an enormous, green snake. She has two horns on top of her head. She has wrapped her body around the hull of the ship.

Suddenly, the ship lurches! You lose your balance and fall. Rockhopper loses his grip on the wheel. He falls forward, hitting his head! You scramble to your feet and run to his side.

"Rockhopper! Are you okay?" you ask.

Rockhopper doesn't answer. He's been knocked out cold. Yarr bounces next to him, upset.

You take a deep breath. It's up to you to save the ship. You look around. How can you stop the sea monster?

You spot a life preserver shooter tied to the rails. Maybe you could use that to lasso the sea monster. You head toward it.

Then you notice something. The sea monster keeps butting her head against the Hold of the ship. She's trying to push her head through a porthole. Does she want something in the Hold?

If you decide to use the life preserver shooter, go to page 20.
If you go down into the Hold to see what the monster wants, go to page 69.

CONTINUED FROM PAGE 35.

You look at the two rocks. You're not sure if you understand the riddle.

"Maybe we should try the iguana path," you say. "All the correct paths might be marked with iguanas."

"Lead the way, matey!" Rockhopper says. "If you're wrong, we can always turn back."

You head down the path. Green zucchini plants grow on either side of you. The path dips down a hill and then . . .

"Aaaaaah!" you scream as you all fall into a deep pit. You, Rockhopper, and Yarr land safely on the bottom.

"It's too high to climb out," you say.

Rockhopper puts Yarr on top of his head. He bounces once, and then lands outside the pit. Then he hops away.

"Yarr will fetch the lizards," Rockhopper says. "They'll come help us."

You hope Rockhopper is right. You don't want to be stuck in that pit forever!

THE END

CONTINUED FROM PAGE 29.

"What does that mean, 'blown off course'?" you ask.

"That's sailor speak for bein' lost," Rockhopper answers. He looks you over. "But I guess ye aren't a real sailor, are ye?"

"I could be a sailor," you say boldly.

"Then go to me quarters and fetch a sextant," he says. "Ye do know what that is?"

"Sure," you say confidently—even though you're not so sure. This is your chance to impress Rockhopper, you think. If you can prove to him you're a good sailor, maybe he won't bring you back to Club Penguin.

You salute Rockhopper. "Aye, aye, Captain!" Then you waddle down the stairs into his quarters. You look around.

Sextant, sextant. It must be something Rockhopper can use to get the ship on course.

There are piles of objects stacked around the room. You spot a friendship bracelet, a puffle bed, even a gold crown. Then you see a strange-looking instrument sticking out of Rockhopper's dresser.

It's a round circle of brass on a piece of wood that kind of looks like a clock. There are numbers around the brass circle, and words like STORMY and VERY DRY written next to the numbers. You pick it up. It might be the sextant, but you're not sure.

You work your way across the room. There is another brass instrument on Rockhopper's desk. This one doesn't look like anything you've ever seen before. It's shaped like a slice of pizza, and there is small, tiny telescope-like thing attached to it, and something that looks like a magnifying glass.

You examine both instruments carefully. Neither of them is marked "sextant." But they're the only things you can find that look like sailors' instruments. You have to bring one to Rockhopper—but which one?

If you choose the item you found in the dresser, go to page 74.
If you choose the item you found on the desk, go to page 65.

CONTINUED FROM PAGE 40.

"Let's surf!" you say bravely. You grab one of the logs.

Yarr leads the way. The little red puffle shows off by doing somersaults as it surfs down the falls. Rockhopper goes next.

"Anchors aweigh!" he cries.

You take a deep breath. You really don't want to do this. But the iguanas are gaining on you.

You hear sounds of "*Zoom! Zoom! Kicky! Kicky!*" getting closer and closer.

"Here goes," you say. You balance on your log, and push off from the top of the falls.

Whoosh! You're glad you like to play *Catchin' Waves*, because you make it to the bottom without wiping out.

The iguanas aren't as brave as you. They stand at the top of the falls, angrily shaking their zucchinis.

"Smartly now! Back to the ship!" Rockhopper cries.

Soon you're all safely on the *Migrator*, sailing away from the strange iguana island.

"Thank ye for rescuin' me," Rockhopper says. "Normally, I'd take a stowaway like ye right back to Club Penguin. But I'd like to reward ye with a little jaunt on the *Migrator*. I'm headed to an island filled with beautiful sand—the same sand I use for me *Treasure Hunt* game. Want to come with me?"

"Of course!" you say. You know you'll be going back to Club Penguin soon—but at least you'll have one more adventure before you're home!

THE END

CONTINUED FROM PAGE 24.

"Choose the pit!" you say.

"Aye, the pit it is!" Rockhopper agrees.

The turtles begin to chant. "Pit! Pit! Pit!"

The Host leads you to the pit. You peer inside. The pit is filled with hundreds—no, thousands—of gold wristwatches.

"By my beard, that's a fine item!" Rockhopper says. "I sold a mess o' these on Club Penguin once. I can bring more of them back! Everyone will love 'em."

"And I can help," you say hopefully.

Rockhopper puts his arm around you. "Of course you can, matey!"

You say good-bye to the strange sea turtles and head for Club Penguin. When you dock, Rockhopper lets you work in his shop. Your friends are impressed to see you working for Rockhopper! But most of all, they're happy you're home again.

THE END

CONTINUED FROM PAGE 14.

You take the path on the right. The path takes you down a steep hill. When you get to the bottom, you find yourself at the mouth of a cave. You peer inside. It's as black as night in there.

Fruit doesn't grow in caves, of course. You should probably turn back and keep looking. But then you remember all of the pirate stories you've read. In the stories, caves always hold amazing treasures.

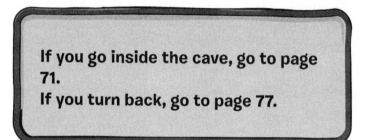

If you go inside the cave, go to page 71.
If you turn back, go to page 77.

CONTINUED FROM PAGE 11.

You shimmy up the mast as fast as you can. The moon shines down on the Crow's Nest, a round platform. Rockhopper's jolly roger flag flies from a pole—it's a black-and-white flag with a puffle and crossbones on it. You see a cannon and a pile of snowballs ready for firing. You curl up next to the cannon and fall asleep.

You wake to the sensation of something bouncing on your belly. It's Yarr! He seems excited to see you.

"Yarr, shhhh!" you say. You reach into your pocket and dig out a cookie. "Here, have a treat!"

Yarr quickly grabs the cookie in his teeth, tosses it around like a Frisbee, catches it, and chows down on it. Then he yawns. The party must have tired him out, too. He curls up with you and you both fall asleep.

When you wake up, the sun is shining. You look down and see that Rockhopper has landed on an island. Rockhopper steps from the ship onto the sandy shore.

"Yarr, where are ye?" Rockhopper calls out.

Suddenly, a group of tiny creatures rushes out from behind a group of rocks on the island. They look like iguanas! They're all wearing grass skirts. They swarm Rockhopper and tie a rope around him. There are too many— Rockhopper can't fight them off. They start to carry him off into the jungle.

You know you have to help Rockhopper— fast. Yarr jumps into the cannon. He wants you to shoot him down into the iguanas to help Rockhopper! It's a good idea, but you wonder what will happen when Yarr lands. Will he be able to handle all those iguanas by himself? Maybe you'd better go with him.

If you and Yarr follow the iguanas together, go to page 30.
If you shoot Yarr out of the cannon, go to page 32.

CONTINUED FROM PAGE 35.

"I remember this riddle from *The Club Penguin Times*," you say. "The answer is a table. Get it? It's got four legs but can't walk."

"Aargh! That's right!" Rockhopper says.

You go down the path marked by a table. The path winds through the fields of zucchini.

"This whole island must be covered with zucchini plants," you say. "Those iguanas must really love that vegetable!"

"It be a tasty treat," Rockhopper agrees. "But I prefer a seaweed pizza myself."

The path forks again. Like before, each path is marked with a rock. One shows a picture of a snake, the other shows a river.

"Read the riddle, matey," Rockhopper says.

"'I run, but have no legs,'" you say. "Hmm."

If you choose the path marked by a snake, go to page 19.
If you choose the path marked by a river, go to page 36.

"Captain Rockhopper, look starboard!" you say.

Rockhopper looks to the right. "What's that strange shining over there?" he asks.

"I think it's Morse code," you say. "It looks like a signal for help. S-O-S."

"Good work, matey," Rockhopper says. "And how does a young penguin like yourself know Morse code?"

"I read a lot of books about ships and sailing," you explain.

Rockhopper nods. "Let's go see who needs our help!"

"What about your mission to find those islands full of treasure?" you ask.

"A sailor never turns his back on another sailor in need," Rockhopper answers. "The treasure can wait."

He sails the *Migrator* toward the light and soon a tiny island comes into view. As you get closer, you see a sea turtle standing on shore! He's using a small mirror to reflect sunlight to make the signal.

Rockhopper anchors the ship and you follow him onto shore. The turtle is happy to see you. His pale green skin has a pattern of brown spots on it. He is wearing a red shirt with holes in it. It looks like he has been on the island for a long time.

"Oh, thank you for coming to my rescue!" the sea turtle says. "I'm very lost, and I don't know how to get back to my island."

"No problem, matey," Rockhopper says. "You can sail aboard me ship. We'll take a look at me charts and see if we can get you home."

The grateful sea turtle follows you aboard. Rockhopper turns to you. "All right, sailor. I'll be belowdecks with our guest. Set the sails so we can head out soon."

"Aye, aye, Captain!" you say.

Rockhopper leaves you on deck. You look up at the ship's sails. Yarr is bouncing up and down on the mast. You may have read a lot of books about sailing, but you have no idea how to set the sails by yourself.

You think about asking Yarr for help. But if Rockhopper finds out, he'll know you're not a real sailor.

If you try to set the sails yourself, go to page 16.

If you ask Yarr to help you with the sails, go to page 22.

CONTINUED FROM PAGE 42.

You decide to jump out of the porthole, in case Shellbeard has a guard stationed by the door. It's not far from shore; you should be able to swim.

You jump out and splash into the water. You start to swim for shore when you hear voices from the deck. You look up to see Shellbeard directing his crew to sail toward the *X*-marks-the-spot on the map.

"Soon the treasure will be ours. Ooogh!"

You can't let Shellbeard get the treasure. A strange feeling of bravery fills you, and you reach for a rope dangling over the side of the ship. You shimmy up and stand on the rail.

"I'll take that map, thank you!" you say, and you grab the map from Shellbeard's hand.

"Stop him!" Shellbeard cries.

You somersault off of the rail and charge down the gangplank, grabbing one of Shellbeard's jet packs you see as you go. Before the pirates can stop you, you jet away from the ship. Soon you see the *Migrator* in the distance. You land on deck.

Rockhopper is surprised to see you. "What happened to you, matey? And where's that turtle?"

You tell Rockhopper the whole story and hand him back the map. He is impressed.

"Does this mean I can join your crew?" you ask.

"Of course not," Rockhopper says. "Yarr is the only crew I need. But I tell ye what—ye can steer the ship back to Club Penguin!"

"Awesome!" you reply. It's too bad you can't be on the crew. But getting to steer the *Migrator* is really cool!

THE END

CONTINUED FROM PAGE 31.

You decide to take the sparkly stones. If they're valuable, Rockhopper can always trade them for fruit, can't he?

You fill your sack with stones and head back to the ship. Rockhopper and Yarr are there. Rockhopper has found the sextant he needs. He asks you if you found any fruit.

"I found something even better," you say, and you spill the stones out onto the deck. Rockhopper grins.

"Aye, that's a fine catch!" he says. "I know an island where I can trade these stones for crates of pirate bandanas. What do ye say? Should we go? We won't get back to Club Penguin for weeks."

"Anchors aweigh, Captain!" you reply, giving him a salute. It might be a long time before you get home again. But your adventure is just beginning!

THE END

CONTINUED FROM PAGE 30.

You decide to pick the lock of the cage. You quietly waddle up. Rockhopper looks startled.

"Shhh," you tell Rockhopper. "I'm here to rescue you."

"But matey—" Rockhopper says.

His warning is too late. A small group of iguanas grabs you! They carry you to another cage and lock the door. You rattle the bars, but they don't even budge. The cage is pretty strong.

"Uh, sorry," you say to Rockhopper. "I stowed away on your ship. And now I can't even rescue you."

"That's all right, matey," Rockhopper says. "We'll find a way out of here. What kind of a pirate would I be if I couldn't escape a bunch of blimey lizards?"

You hope Rockhopper is right. You stowed away on the *Migrator* so you could have an adventure. Though being captured and put in a cage isn't exactly what you had in mind!

THE END

CONTINUED FROM PAGE 24.

"Choose the hut!" you say.

"Aye! The hut it is!" Rockhopper yells.

The Host leads you to the hut. You hope to find gold and treasure inside. The Host opens the hut to reveal . . . another turtle! He is wearing a T-shirt that says GUIDE on it.

"You have won the services of our Guide. He is the greatest Guide in the seven seas!" your Host says. "The Guide will take you wherever you want to go."

Rockhopper's eyes light up. "Anywhere? Tell me, lad, have ye heard of a chain of islands shaped like an anchor? Can you take us there?"

The Guide points to his T-shirt. "I'm a Guide, aren't I?"

So the Guide follows you onboard the *Migrator* as the turtles cheer you on. The Guide plots a course and the ship sails for three days. On the morning of the third day, you climb into the Crow's Nest with Yarr. The puffle lets you look through the telescope.

"I see them!" you yell. "There's a bunch of islands, and they're shaped like an anchor!"

You climb down as the island chain comes into view. Rockhopper turns to the Guide.

"Okay, matey, now guide us to the treasure," he says.

The Guide looks confused. "Hey, I'm not a treasure hunter. My shirt says 'Guide,' not 'Pirate.' Finding treasure is your job."

"Ye mean ye don't know the passageway into the island chain?" Rockhopper asks.

The Guide shrugs. "Nope. I just know how to get here."

Rockhopper looks through a telescope. "Let's see. The islands are all close together. We'll have to look for a passageway to get through them. Should we start at the bottom, or head for the top first? What do ye think?"

Rockhopper looks at you. You feel important—he's asking for your advice! You just hope you make the right choice.

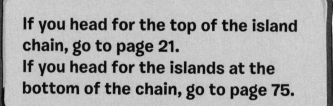

If you head for the top of the island chain, go to page 21.
If you head for the islands at the bottom of the chain, go to page 75.

CONTINUED FROM PAGE 48.

You think the clock-like instrument might
be something called a barometer, a tool used for
predicting the weather. So you decide to bring
the pizza-shaped instrument with you.

Rockhopper spots you coming up the stairs.
"Good work! That's me sextant, all right!"

You are excited that you got it right, and
run toward Rockhopper.

Slam! You slip on the wet deck and fall
right on your beak. The sextant flies out of your
flipper—and breaks!

Rockhopper sighs. "That's all right," he
says. "I can steer by the stars. We'll lower our
sails until nightfall."

You feel terrible about the broken sextant.
You ask Rockhopper what you can do to help,
and he puts you to work. You scrub the decks.
You polish Rockhopper's snowball-shooting
cannon up in the Crow's Nest. You clean up all
of the items that moved around during the storm.
Rockhopper stays busy looking at charts and
maps in his office.

Night falls, and you follow Rockhopper on

deck. Yarr hops up to the Crow's Nest to act as lookout. But the sky is filled with hazy clouds.

"No stars tonight," Rockhopper says. "Maybe we'll have better luck tomorrow."

Suddenly, Yarr jumps down from the Crow's Nest and bounces excitedly. You look out over the water and see a dark figure rise up, and then dive back under the surface. It's too big to be a dolphin, and isn't shaped like a whale.

"I hope that's not what I think it is," Rockhopper says.

"What do you mean?" you ask.

"It was a night just like this one," Rockhopper says. "I was at sea when a dark shadow crossed me ship. It was a sea monster! Terrible it was, with green, scaly skin. It was swimming right for the *Migrator*! But I got lucky, and a swift wind whipped up. I sailed away as fast as I could."

"That sounds dangerous," you say.

"A pirate never shies away from danger, matey," Rockhopper replies. "A sense of adventure is a pirate's most important tool. More important than an eye patch or a fancy hat, even. And don't you forget that."

There's no more sign of the dark figure in the water, so Rockhopper sets you up in a comfortable hammock for the night. You dream of sea monsters. In the morning, you're awakened by Rockhopper shouting, "Land ho!"

You jump out of the hammock and run up on deck. The ship is right in front of an island.

"Maybe I can find some sailing equipment here," Rockhopper says. "You might want to stay here, just to be safe."

You think about the sea monster and think that sounds like a good idea. Who knows what strange creatures live on that island? But as you watch Rockhopper and Yarr leave, you feel an itch to go along. You've never been to another island before. Maybe you should catch up to Rockhopper and ask if you can go along.

If you follow Rockhopper onto the island, go to page 13.
If you stay onboard, go to page 76.

"Let's take the path on the left," you say.

"All righty, matey!" Rockhopper agrees.

You head down the path, which leads to the edge of the zucchini fields. Your heart starts to pound as you see a big treasure chest in the distance.

"It's the treasure!" you shout, and you charge toward it.

You wait until Rockhopper and Yarr catch up before you open the lid.

Inside the treasure chest are . . . hundreds and hundreds of zucchini!

"Oh no!" you wail.

Rockhopper laughs. "'Tis a mighty fine treasure if you're a zucchini-lovin' lizard," he says. "Don't be sad, matey. Not every adventure ends in treasure. Most times, the adventure you have is the best treasure of all."

You know Rockhopper is right. Your adventure with Rockhopper has been one you will never forget!

THE END

CONTINUED FROM PAGE 45.

You race down into the Hold. The sea monster has pushed her head through the porthole.

ROAR! She is straining toward something— the bag of green fruit! But she can't reach it.

You bravely run to the sack of fruit. You start tossing the fruit into the sea monster's mouth. She gobbles it up, then smiles.

ROAR! she says, but this time she sounds happy, not angry. She swims away from the ship, and the *Migrator* is calm once again.

You go back up on deck. Rockhopper is sitting up, rubbing his head.

"What happened?" he asks.

You tell him how you fed the green fruit to the sea monster.

"Excellent thinking, matey!" Rockhopper congratulates you. "You'll make a great sailor yet. Tell you what. Let's not go back to Club Penguin yet. We can sail for new horizons in the morning."

The offer is tempting. But between storms and sea monsters, you've had enough adventure. You really want a slice of seaweed pizza and a nice, calm game of *Find Four*.

"No thanks," you say. "It was fun being a pirate for a little while. But I think I'd like to go back to Club Penguin."

THE END

CONTINUED FROM PAGE 52.

Your sense of adventure has taken you this far. You might as well let it take you into the cave! You take a deep breath and head inside.

Your eyes slowly adjust to the darkness. It reminds you of being in the Mine Shack back on Club Penguin. You seem to be going down deeper into the ground with each step. You start to shiver. It's chilly underground!

Suddenly, you hear a voice. "Who goes there?"

"A pirate!" you call out. "Who are you?"

A figure steps out of the shadows. It's a penguin! He's blue, and has a long, white beard and a pink and yellow hat on his head. You have seen this hat on only a few penguins before—it's a Beta Hat. Only penguins who were part of Club Penguin from the very start own that hat.

"Well, what do you know!" the old penguin says. "Are you from Club Penguin?"

"Yes, but now I sail with Captain Rockhopper on the *Migrator*," you say proudly.

"I can go home at last!" the penguin says.

"Are you from Club Penguin, too?" you ask.

The old penguin begins his story. "I was young like you, once. I liked living on Club Penguin, but I always wondered what lands waited for me beyond the waves. So I built myself a boat and set sail. But a storm kicked up, and I have been stranded here on this island ever since. I missed Club Penguin's snow and ice, so I live down here in the cave, where it's cool."

You have an idea. "Did you have any sailing tools on your boat?" you ask.

The old penguin nods, holding up a funny but familiar-looking object. "I managed to save my sextant, but without a boat, it's no use to me."

"Follow me," you say. You take the penguin to meet Rockhopper. He is happy to have the tool he needs, and he is happy to bring the old penguin home.

"Thank you," says the old penguin. "I can't wait to see Club Penguin again!"

You can't wait to go home, either. Talking with the shipwrecked penguin has made you realize how much you miss it. And now you have a great story to tell your buddies!

THE END

CONTINUED FROM PAGE 38.

"What's the worst vegetable to have on a ship?" you ask Rockhopper.

Rockhopper looks at you. "I don't know, matey. What?"

"A *leek*!" you say. "Leek! Get it?"

Rockhopper chuckles. "Aye, you're right!" he says. "Listen, matey. I'm sorry I can't let ye stay on me ship. It's for your own good."

"I understand," you say. At least you tried.

Soon you're back on Club Penguin. Penguins have seen the *Migrator* in the telescope. They're gathered at the Beach and they're surprised to see you come off the ship!

"Good-bye, matey!" Rockhopper calls to you. Then he sails away.

Other penguins crowd around you.

"Did you really sail on the *Migrator*?"

"What's Rockhopper like?"

"Will you be my buddy?"

You smile. You've just had the experience of a lifetime!

THE END

You choose the instrument that looks like a clock and bring it to Rockhopper.

"Matey, that's me barometer!" Rockhopper says. "It's an instrument for measurin' the weather. I'll get the sextant myself."

Rockhopper heads down to his quarters, and you feel sad. You had one chance to impress Rockhopper, and you blew it!

Rockhopper comes back on deck holding the sextant—the instrument shaped like a pizza slice. He also has a small box with him.

"Thanks for finding me barometer," he says. "I lost it weeks ago. Take this rare item as a token of me appreciation."

He hands you the box. There's a gold wristwatch inside! Rockhopper brought a bunch of them to sell on Club Penguin once. But you never got one.

Rockhopper sets course for Club Penguin, but you're not sad anymore. You can't wait to get home and show your buddies what Rockhopper gave you!

THE END

CONTINUED FROM PAGE 64.

"Let's try the lower part," you suggest.

Rockhopper nods and steers the ship around the islands in the bottom of the chain. The route curves and lo and behold, you see a wide passageway between two of the islands. You've found it!

Rockhopper steers the ship into the passageway, and you soon see why these islands are legendary. On the outside, all you can see are tall trees. But once inside you can see that the shores of each island are filled with jewels, glittering red, blue, and green in the sun.

"These will be perfect for me *Treasure Hunt* game," Rockhopper says. "Thank you for gettin' us here."

The Guide shrugs. "Hey, that's what I do. That's why I get to wear the shirt!"

You help Rockhopper load up his ship with the treasure and set sail for Club Penguin. With Rockhopper and his bounty, you're going to make an exciting return home!

THE END

CONTINUED FROM PAGE 67.

You decide to stay onboard and keep cleaning the ship. Maybe this will impress Rockhopper.

But while you are cleaning up, you trip over a pink flamingo lawn ornament. You fall backward into the stack of cream soda barrels. The stack of barrels falls apart, and they roll all around the Hold!

You scramble to grab them, but it's too late. A barrel slams into the side of the ship. The wood splinters, and water begins to pour in.

The ship is sinking! You panic. You quickly grab an inflatable raft and run up on deck. You drop the raft into the water and jump in. As the waves carry the raft away, you watch the ship slowly sink into the waves.

You feel awful! Rockhopper and Yarr might be stranded on the island. And you're not even sure how to get back to Club Penguin!

You wish you had never stowed away on Rockhopper's ship.

THE END

CONTINUED FROM PAGE 52.

It's tempting to go into the cave, but Rockhopper gave you a job to do, and you don't want to fail. You trudge back up the hill.

You're about to go on the left-hand path when you notice a third one between the two. One of the big pink flowers is blocking it, but you push it aside and see a narrow path ahead. You decide to take the new path.

You have to keep pushing aside the big flowers as you walk. Finally the path comes to a dead end. There's nothing but a big clump of the flowers ahead of you. You frown. What a waste of time!

You're about to turn back when you notice a gleam behind the flowers. You close in to investigate and push aside the leaves and stems. Then you gasp.

The flowers have grown around a treasure chest filled with gold coins!

"Woo hoo!" you yell. Then you run to find Rockhopper.

The captain and Yarr are on their way back to the boat.

"Good news," Rockhopper says. "I found a small port. I was able to buy a sextant there. Now we can go back to Club Penguin."

"I have good news, too!" you say. "Follow me!"

Rockhopper and Yarr are thrilled to see the chest of gold coins.

"Good work, matey!" Rockhopper says. "Tell ye what. I'll let ye keep half the coins for yerself. How does that grab ye?"

"That's awesome!" you reply. Now you can't wait to get back to Club Penguin. You've been wanting to upgrade your igloo. And you've had your eye on a big-screen TV for ages now. With your new riches, you'll have one of the coolest igloos on Club Penguin!

THE END

CONTINUED FROM PAGE 40.

"I don't think I can surf that waterfall," you say.

"Then we'll take the path," Rockhopper says.

The path leads downhill, past fields and fields of zucchini. The iguanas are following you. You can hear them getting closer.

Things look hopeless when the path ends at the edge of a cliff hanging ten feet above the ocean. You peer over the cliff. Three dolphins are sticking their heads out of the water.

"Ah, me ocean friends," Rockhopper says. "It's time to hitch a ride, mateys!"

You all jump into the water with a splash. One of the dolphins swims next to you, and you climb up onto its back. Then the three dolphins swim away from the island and take you to the *Migrator*.

As you climb aboard the ship, you are tired and wet, but happy. You helped rescue Rockhopper, and you got to ride a dolphin! Your buddies will never believe your stories.

THE END

CONTINUED FROM PAGE 18.

You run upstairs as fast as you can. Rockhopper is fixing the sails.

"Captain!" you cry. "That sea turtle is really a pirate named Shellbeard. He stole a treasure map off of your desk and jumped into a getaway boat!"

To your surprise, Rockhopper laughs. "A pirate, eh? Well he's not a very good one then. That's an old treasure map. I've already dug up the treasure there. The only thing Shellbeard is going to find is a big, deep hole!"

You laugh, relieved. "So I guess it's back to Club Penguin, then?" you say.

"In due time," Rockhopper says. "Come down into the Hold with me. I'll show ye some real treasure that'll make your eyes bigger than pizzas!"

"Thanks!" you say, excited. When you get back to Club Penguin, you'll be able to tell your friends about all the secret treasures you've seen. You can hardly wait!

THE END